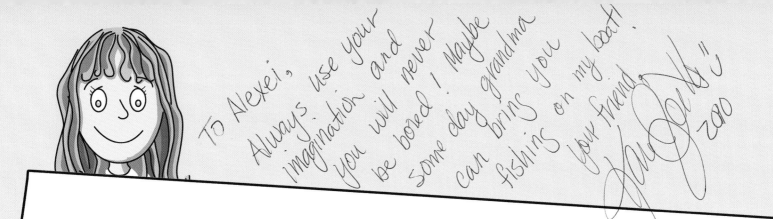

Written by Karen Fenton
Illustrated by Stacy Schulstrom Roth
Harbour Arts, LLC.
Florida

www.harbourarts.com

Library of Congress Cataloging-in-Publication Data
Fenton, Karen. It's raining outside and I'm gonna be bored/ by Karen Fenton;
Illustrated by Stacy Schulstrom Roth. p. cm.
"Harbour Arts, LLC."
Summary: A little girl and her dog look for adventure inside their house
on a rainy day.

ISBN 0-9778196-4-7

Library of Congress (CIP)

10 9 8 7 6 5 4 3 2 1

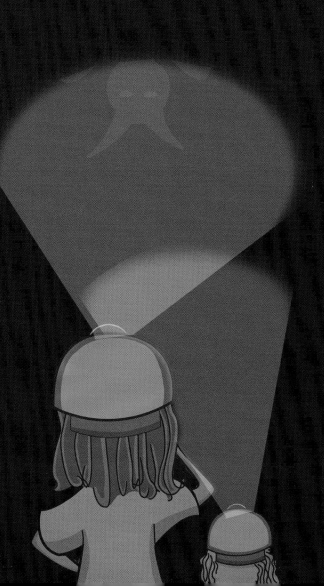

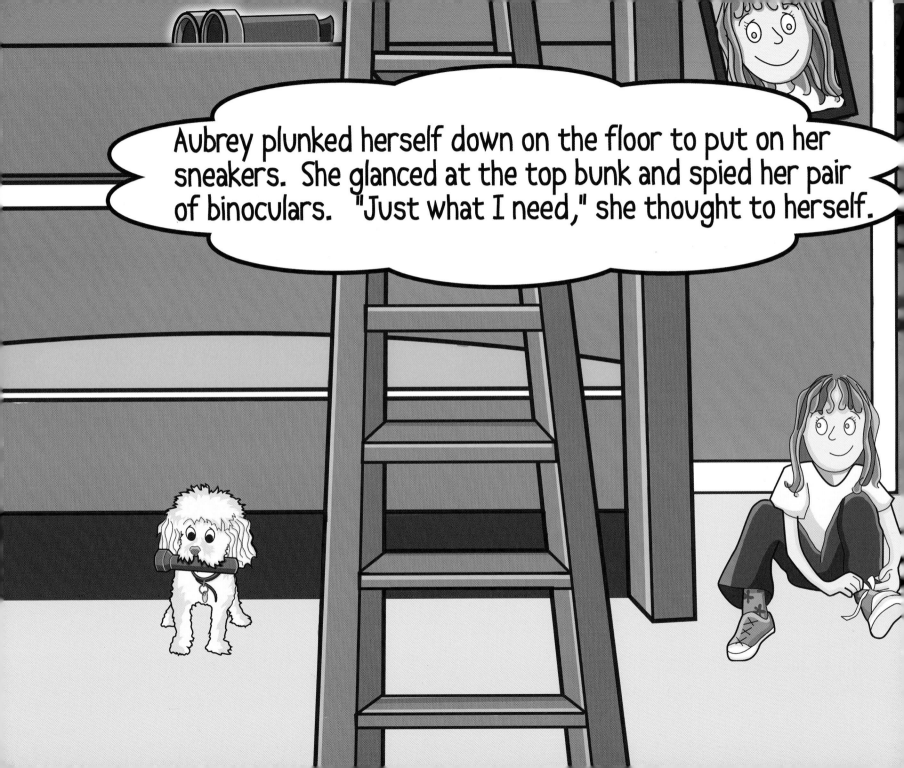

Soon, she bounded off her bed like a paratrooper jumping from an airplane.

The flowing warm waters of the Great Barrier Reef in Australia felt wonderful as Aubrey drifted effortlessly among the coral.

wearily slipped on her pajamas,
and slowly crawled under the covers. "Maybe today
wasn't as boring as I thought it would be," reflected
Aubrey, as memories of her exciting adventures
filled her dreams.